Kaya Wants To Get Ahead

Copyright: © 2005 Baumhaus Verlag, Frankfurt am Main, Germany
Original title: KAYA, FREI UND STARK – KAYA WILL NACH VORN
Cover and inside illustrations: Baumhaus Verlag
Printed in Germany, 2007
Translated by Karen Nickel Anhalt
Typeset by Roberta L. Melzl
Editor: Bobbie Chase

ISBN: 1-933343-63-X

Stabenfeldt, Inc.
457 North Main Street
Danbury, CT 06811
www.pony.us

Gaby Hauptmann

Kaya Wants To Get Ahead

Translated by Karen Nickel Anhalt

For Jella, my sweet niece
"Horse sense is the sense a horse has which
keeps it from betting on people."
– Oscar Wilde

Flying Dream was already a little rounder. Living the life of a privately owned pony and not being ridden by a different girl each day obviously agreed with him. By order of his new owner, Mr. Walden, he went out on the paddock in the morning, where he rollicked about with the other ponies and nibbled on grass with great pleasure. He didn't have to return to the stable until Charlotte came to ride him or Kaya came to train him.

Thirteen-year-old Kaya had ridden Dreamy, a dark brown pony with lyrically beautiful eyes, at the Pony Cup in Franklin. She took third place in the show jumping course at the national riding tournament. No one had expected anything like that, least of all Kaya. But all of a sudden, Dreamy was put up for sale, supposedly because a twelve-year-old pony couldn't be rented out forever. In addition, his market value had shot up dramatically after placing so well in Franklin. Whatever, Kaya and her friends didn't want Dreamy to end up with strangers, so they devised a spectacular plan to kidnap him. It all turned out okay in the end, though, because Mr. Walden had bought Dreamy for his ten-year-old daughter, Charlotte. And he wanted Kaya to continue training him. The coolest part of all in the whole deal was Charlotte's brother, Chris, the 15-year-old guy who also started in Franklin. Unlike Kaya, however, he had bad luck there. Although he was riding the better pony, at the last oxer he knocked the top pole off. That didn't matter to Kaya, though; she thought Chris was cute. And she had to admit that she had a little crush on him, too.

But how could she get Chris to fall for her too? She tried nearly every trick she could think of, but all her attempts to get a little closer to him were as unsuccessful as Chris had been in Franklin. Luckily though, since she was training Dreamy, she was practically a part of the family now. They even rode to tournaments together. She was grateful to Charlotte for that ... even if she was a little bratty.

On this particular day, Kaya went down to the stable later than usual. Her mother had forced her to help out in the garden, something she couldn't stand doing. Mowing the lawn was unbearably boring and seemed totally pointless, because the grass grew back so quickly. On top of that, she had a serious problem with mowing whenever there were little daisies or other pretty wildflowers growing on the lawn. Should she heartlessly kill them all? Kaya couldn't bring herself to do that, so she mowed around them. As a result the lawn looked even worse than before.

When Kaya finished, her mother just raised her eyebrows and shook her head. Then she had to dash back into the restaurant because it was packed with people who wanted to take advantage of the late summer sunshine to enjoy coffee and cake outside on the terrace.

Kaya was glad that her mother didn't have any time because her lectures were always a nightmare. If her big sister Alexa were around, things were even worse because Alexa was of the opinion that she was always right, simply because she was older. Kaya headed straight for the paddock. Her friend Mia, who had her own pony, was already there. She sat on the paddock fence and watched the horses as they rubbed each other at the withers and shooed annoying flies by vigorously swinging their tails.

"Hi Mia," said Kaya as she sat down next to her on the highest rail. "Have you been waiting long?"

"No big deal," Mia shrugged her shoulders. "It's fun watching our little fellows. Dreamy just dawdles around while Luxy constantly tries to challenge him. Dreamy will join in for a little while, but then he gives up just as quickly. I have a feeling that he thinks it's a big waste of energy that he could better use for something else."

Mia, a delicate 13-year-old girl, took second place at Franklin in show jumping with Luxury Illusion, one place ahead of Kaya and Dreamy. Her pony was a marvelous gray horse – a remarkably talented and cooperative jumper, a real rascal on four legs. But then again, Mia's father had the time to drive to the top trainers in the region, to special training courses and to the tournaments. Kaya's parents, on the other hand, worked in their restaurant from morning until evening. Her mother served their guests while her father ran the kitchen. The closest they ever got to a tournament was watching the video Mia's father once made of Kaya riding. On top of that, over the last few years they had invested so much money in their house and the restaurant attached to it that there wasn't much money left over for an expensive hobby like horses. Anyway, Kaya wasn't jealous of Mia. Things were the way they were. And it was okay that Chris's father had a lot more money, too. After all, he was able to buy Dreamy with that money.

"Are you planning to ride today?" asked Mia.

"Yes, Charlotte doesn't have the time today. She told me why – but I forgot."

Mia was quiet for a minute. Then she looked into Kaya's eyes. "Do you like her?"

Kaya thought about that. Charlotte was nice and bubbled over with enthusiasm and good spirits. But as soon as the least little thing went wrong or didn't go exactly the way she wanted it to, her mood soured. Then she could be really prickly or totally whiney so that you didn't know how to react: Sympathetically? Angrily? Annoyed? Soothingly?

"She's okay." Kaya hesitated. "But sometimes a little exhausting."

Mia nodded and was silent for a while.

"If I had an extra pony, I'd give it to you," she said.

Kaya put her arm around her shoulders. "You are a true friend!"

"Yes, but I only have Luxy!"

Kaya had saddled up Dreamy, but she could only buckle the girth in the last hole, thanks to his round, grass-filled belly.

Then she led him into the riding hall, where Claudia was giving lessons. Claudia was not only the riding teacher, but was, together with her husband, the owner of the stable, too. The hall was small but modern. It had lots of windows that let in the light.

At the front end, there was a small clubhouse for the riders which Claudia had added on.

Dreamy seemed tired. Either that, or he just wasn't in the mood – it was all a matter of perspective. Kaya thought he was just lazy and she knew the reasons why. For one thing, frolicking on the paddock in the warm weather took a lot out of you. Besides, after all that fun it was obvious that Dreamy's opinion of a dressage lesson was the same as her opinion of an English class: hopelessly boring. When he got into the arena and didn't see any obstacles, well, he just didn't bother trying.

"Hey, act a little bit more like a dressage pony, please," Kaya cajoled him as she trotted through her first rounds with him. "Come on, pretend that you're a top-rated pony with an excellent walk and such a strong trot that the people in the stands hold their breaths when they watch you. Show me a proud posture that even an Andalusian would hide behind!"

Dreamy turned his ears back attentively, but then stumbled clumsily over his own legs.

"Oh great," sighed Kaya. She looked out of the window at the clubhouse just as the door opened and a tall man walked in. He sat down at one of the tables and faced the arena. Kaya looked him over one more time, but there was no doubt that it was Mr. Walden, Dreamy's owner. "Oh great," Kaya sighed again. Today of all days. Now she had to try especially hard ... hopefully it would work out.

There were only four riders in the hall. Mia rode Luxy and Reni was on a Norwegian that she cared for and, in exchange, was allowed to ride occasionally. Cindy sat on a small pony that belonged to the club. They were all friends. Only Freddy was missing, but she was on vacation with her parents. Fortunately they still had another week of summer vacation before they had to go back to the daily grind at school.

"Hey there, you Wild Amazons," said Claudia as she began her lesson, looking over each of the girls. She sometimes called them that as a joke – it was the name they'd given themselves when they'd kidnapped Dreamy.

"Okay, you can start trotting!"

Dreamy grumbled crankily as he felt Kaya's command to trot. But Kaya wanted to make a good impression now, so she concentrated on her position and tried to guide him with the reins, just as Claudia was always telling her. During the course of the lesson, Dreamy gave up his resistance and worked with her. He was smart enough to know that the decision about how many carrots or snacks he would get would be made at the end of the lesson. Shortly before it was over, he crossed the track in a strong trot, throwing his legs so high and responding with such decisiveness that Kaya thought she was dreaming. What was up with him? The others were just as amazed.

Claudia waved over to the window. *Of course*, thought Kaya to herself, *Claudia knew that Mr. Walden would be coming. That's why she told me to be especially fastidious in grooming Dreamy.* At the time Kaya felt insulted, as if Claudia were questioning her honor or something. But in hindsight, it was a good thing. Otherwise she wouldn't have been so thorough after Dreamy's *intermezzo* on the paddock.

When the lesson was over, Mia rode up alongside her and said with astonishment, "Maybe he isn't a jumping pony after all, but an intermediate!"

Kaya had to laugh. "Considering that at the start of the lesson he could barely bring himself to set one hoof in front of the other, he was truly incredible!"

She patted Dreamy's neck and enjoyed the moment. There's not much that's as enjoyable as letting the reigns slacken after a good lesson and riding alongside your friends, chatting. Dreamy was sweating and Kaya breathed in the scent and was happy.

"Isn't that Mr. Walden in the clubroom?" asked Reni, who had joined them on her Norwegian horse. "Do you suppose he just happened to stop by?"

Kaya threw a glance in his direction. No doubt he wanted to stay abreast of her level of accomplishment. After all, the first tournament that Charlotte would be starting in with Dreamy was just two weeks away.

"What do you think?" asked Kaya.

"He's a businessman. He didn't just stop by to say hello!"

Kaya thought it over and figured that Reni was right. Since buying Dreamy, Mr. Walden had only visited the stable two times. Once to see how the spring jumping training was progressing and another time when Charlotte jumped with Dreamy for the first time.

But for him to stop by for an ordinary dressage lesson, without any special trainer or anything, well, that really was odd.

"You're right," said Kaya. "I doubt he's just come by for a friendly chat."

After she had taken care of Dreamy, Kaya looked

around for Mr. Walden's car. His big black BMW was still in the parking lot. The car really stood out since this was not a fancy place, but a small stable that had been built up to its current size over the course of many years. Most of the cars parked here were worn and beat up, nothing luxurious at all.

Kaya went back to the riding hall and peeked into the clubhouse room. He sat there with a glass of cola that Claudia had no doubt poured for him, and they were just clinking their glasses together in a toast. Could they be having a little tête-à-tête? Kaya wasn't sure what she should do.

She knocked on the door.

Mr. Walden looked up and instantly recognized her through the square window in the door and waved to her. Kaya went in and shook his hand.

"You rode wonderfully!" he said. His praise made her happy, although she knew that the exceptional finish was exclusively the accomplishment of Dreamy. He was a joker and had showed them once again just how much he was capable of when he felt like it.

"Thanks," she said simply, and kept her thoughts to herself.

Mr. Walden was a big man. He seemed to be a little

older than her father, although he probably wasn't
– she figured he looked that way because of the
suits and ties that he wore all the time, as if he were
permanently on a business trip.

"Why don't you have a seat?" he said and Claudia
smiled at her in a way that made Kaya suspicious.
What were the two of them scheming together?

"You know my son," began Mr. Walden. Suddenly
her heart started beating more quickly. She hadn't
seen Chris in over a week. Considering the size of her
crush on him, that was an eternity.

She nodded, but couldn't say anything. Her heart
was pounding and her pulse was way up. What was
all this about? Did they want to trade Dreamy in or
sell him again? After all that had transpired, that
would be a scandal!

"We've just found a pony in a training stable that
he is really excited about," continued Chris's father.

Another pony! Kaya was surprised, but she
breathed a sigh of relief and was able to speak again.
"And Chris's mare?"

"She's fine, but he only has one more year on the
Pony Squad. After that, he can't start in a tournament
on a pony anymore ... and that's why he'd like to
start on a real fireball next time!"

Well, that was easy for Chris to say, a real fireball. He wants a real fireball, so his parents travel all over Germany to find one and then open their wallets. Did anyone say life was fair? No, probably not.

She nodded again.

"The one he found has already participated in the National championships. And placed."

Kaya swallowed. How could anyone afford a pony like that?

"So why is it up for sale?" she wanted to know.

"Because the girl who rode it turned seventeen, which means that she can't ride it in tournaments any more and has to switch to a horse."

That's how easy it was. When you turn seventeen, your pony is traded in or given away like an old bicycle. Who will bid this, who will offer more? Good grief! She thought about Dreamy and his deep eyes and nodded again.

"Chris thinks that he could really take off with him!"

Was a talented, cooperative horse in reality the unluckiest of horses? It would be passed along as long as it was in good shape – but what then? The average horses did better. They accomplished a little and received a lot of love in return.

"Oh really?" she said because it was so quiet

and Claudia and Mr. Walden were looking at her so intently. Had she missed something?

"But he wants a second opinion," said Mr. Walden. Kaya looked at him, but didn't say a thing. What was she supposed to say to that anyway?

"What Mr. Walden is trying to say is that you should also try him out," explained Claudia.

"Me?" Kaya's mouth went dry. "On a National Championship pony? What am I supposed to do with it?"

Mr. Walden had to laugh. "Maybe you could ride him?"

Kaya swallowed. "And how am I supposed to do that?"

He laughed again. "I think you've already learned that!"

"No, I mean, why? And where? And what is this all about?"

Now both of them laughed, Claudia too.

She must have looked thoroughly perplexed. "We'll ask your parents if it's okay … then you can drive up there with me and stay with us for three days. That should be enough time to test the pony."

Kaya had no idea how to respond, it all sounded so unbelievable. But one thing was already clear to her: she would be spending three days with Chris. A National Championship pony was all well and good, but the situation with Chris was fantastic! Amazing! But did his parents know what they were doing?

She didn't see her own parents until the next day. It was Wednesday, their day off, and they were having a leisurely breakfast in the garden. Her 17-year-old sister, Alexa, also happened to be there. Alexa was an excellent rider and had taken a year off after tenth grade to ride at her uncle's stables. But now she was working on preparing for her college entrance exams so that she could earn a lot of money one day and have her own horses.

"So, kid," said Alexa before she had barely even sat down. "What's up? Is there a conquest you're celebrating?"

Her mother looked at them quizzically. "What's that supposed to mean?"

"How am I supposed to know?" blurted out Kaya with a scowl. Her eyes were in an angry squint and she glowered at her sister. "Ask her yourself!"

It was obvious. Alexa seemed to think that she had generously left Chris to her younger sister by deciding not to date him herself.

"Well?" asked her mother and reached for a freshly baked roll.

"Nothing," said Alexa innocently and shrugged her shoulders. "Could you pass me the honey?"

"It looks like we've got all the wasps in the western hemisphere out here!" laughed her father. He was wearing a red polo shirt and looked young and adventurous. He always came to life on his day off. In the mornings he was bursting with energy and in the afternoons he relaxed in his favorite recliner with a stack of reading material. If it was sunny, he'd do his reading outside. "By the way," he said, pointing at the lawn, "who mowed the lawn? It looks terrible!"

Alexa pointed at Kaya, wordlessly.

"At least I *did* it," said Kaya as she sliced her roll open. "That's not something you'd ever bother with."

"Now, now," her mother said, gazing at the garden with its two fruit trees and wildflowers at the edges, and then at the middle of the lawn, with the islands of high grass with wildflowers. Then she said, "Well, it has a certain panache!" and laughed. "Maybe you are the only real artist in the family!"

Kaya didn't laugh. She was impatient for the subject to turn to the Waldens. Finally she asked, "Has Mr. Walden called yet?"

19

"Of course," said her father. "Didn't you know?"

"How should I know?" snapped Kaya. "If you don't tell me anything, how am I supposed to know?" She tossed her shoulder length dark blonde hair behind her and looked at her father impatiently.

"He's picking you up in about an hour, and you'll be gone for three days. So be sure to pack enough clothes, and especially your toothbrush, pajamas and fresh underwear."

Kaya jumped up so fast that her chair toppled over. "And you waited until now to tell me that?"

"Sit down. You couldn't possibly need an hour to pack your things."

"Of course I need an hour. At least! I'm so excited that I can't even think straight!"

"What's going on?" asked Alexa, raising her eyebrows. Her mother dismissed her question with a wave of her hand. "We'll explain in a minute."

"Oh great," she said. "The brat gets to go away for three days and I get to help in the restaurant."

"It's not like you don't earn anything for helping," said her father.

"Sure, so that I can take a three-day vacation," Alexa replied sarcastically.

The black BMW was gigantic and the inside smelled like new leather. Kaya sunk down in the passenger seat and was dazzled by all the lights and indicators next to the steering wheel. "This looks like an airplane cockpit!" she said in a hushed, respectful voice. Mr. Walden just laughed and looked over to her. "You can raise the seat if you'd like. Here, I'll show you how!" He left the motor on and she waved goodbye to her parents, who were waving to her from the sidewalk. Her father had put his arm around her mother. They looked like a happy young couple.

"You have nice parents," said Mr. Walden as he waved to them while driving off.

"Yes, I'm pretty fond of them," said Kaya, and felt a mix of pride and love. It was true. She didn't spend as much time with them as she would have liked because her parents had to work so much, but they really were great. She could have done a lot worse.

Four hours later, the navigation system indicated that they had reached their destination street.

"Now things are going to get exciting!" Mr. Walden picked up his cell phone and dialed a number. He had been making calls during the entire trip, but they were all business calls that he made on the hands-free system in the car. This time she wasn't supposed to hear what was being said. He was probably calling his wife.

Kaya pretended not to pay attention, but she was much too curious.

"A cabin?" His tone of voice made it obvious that he was not thrilled. "Why not a hotel?"

Kaya looked out the window. Up until now all she had seen was a green meadow. Destination street? Where was it?

"Well that's annoying." She sensed him looking at her. "You could have told me that a little earlier!"

Kaya decided to continue staring out the window.

"I'm not being annoying – I am annoyed. There's a difference!"

Kaya examined her fingernails. Oh great, it sounded like trouble. She wanted to disappear.

"Sure, I'll handle it. See you in a few minutes!"

He let out a deep sigh and needed a few minutes to think before he began to talk. Kaya turned to him.

"My wife is sometimes a little ..." he searched for the right word, "let's say, disorganized. Or better, impulsive. Or maybe spontaneous. Well, whatever, here's the problem. It's summer vacation and all the hotels in the area are totally booked. So it looks like we'll be living in a summer cottage."

He hesitated and then added, almost contemptuously, "In a cabin."

"Cool!" The exclamation just slipped out of Kaya's mouth. Together with Chris in a cabin – that would be really romantic!

"Cool?" asked Mr. Walden and looked at her.

"Yes!" said Kaya. "That'll be much nicer than some sterile hotel!"

He sighed again. "Well, I'm not so sure."

Just at this moment, a huge riding hall came into view. Several smaller buildings were strewn around it.

"Hey, there it is!" cheered Kaya, and was immediately embarrassed. She was so uncool. What must he think of her? They rolled onto a huge asphalt courtyard, the parking spots full with horse transporters.

"Wow!" Kaya was so enthralled that she gave up trying to reign in her emotions. She simply had never seen such an impressive riding stable.

Mr. Walden gave her a smile. "Wait until you see the indoor riding arena. Chris said that it's easily twice as big as ours!"

When he referred to 'ours,' he was talking about the fancy stable where Chris trained. And that meant that it was four times as big as 'her' riding arena.

"Incredible!" she said. "Dreamy would walk himself to death here!"

Mr. Walden laughed again. "Dreamy is a clever fellow – he never does more than he wants to do!"

Aha, so he did have Dreamy's number. She had always thought that unlike his wife, Mr. Walden didn't understand much about horses.

They pulled in between two expensive SUVs. This time Kaya avoided making a comment. She didn't want to come off as a country bumpkin.

"And where's Chris?" she asked instead.

"Riding the pony, according to my wife."

"How exciting!"

The huge entrance door opened into a vestibule, which led to the riding arena. They were greeted by a loud chattering of birds – and a friendly wave from Mrs. Walden, who stood in the open doorway. She smiled and held her pointer finger to her lips. Kaya left Mr. Walden's side and walked over to her quickly.

"How nice that you could come along!" whispered Mrs. Walden. She had pulled her blonde hair into a ponytail, and in her blouse and jeans she almost looked like she could be Chris's older sister.

"I'm so happy to be here, thank you," said Kaya

as she shook her hand. She couldn't resist the urge to look past her into the arena. She saw a course that had obviously been set up exclusively for Chris, because he was the only one riding it. Besides him, the only other person she could see was a big man with broad shoulders, who was obviously in charge.

"You've arrived at exactly the right time," said Mrs. Walden as she gave her husband a quick peck on the cheek and turned back to watching so that she wouldn't miss a thing. "Up until now, the instructor has only allowed Chris to take the individual obstacles, but not the entire course." *And that course is frighteningly high*, thought Kaya.

"What is that? Class M?" she asked.

"Good guess! But it's no problem for Wild Thing. She can go even higher!"

"But that's even taller than she is!" Kaya couldn't bear to look. There was no way this was going to work out. Dreamy would just walk underneath.

"Looks can be deceiving," said Mrs. Walden. She grabbed Kaya's shoulder and said, "Now, watch!"

It started off with a classic log jump. That was pretty harmless, but then came verticals and oxers. The thing that irritated Kaya was the irregular, even random positioning of the obstacles. The combinations in particular seemed to be positioned strangely and without any normal spacing.

But what Mrs. Walden said was true. This 'wild thing' sailed effortlessly over each obstacle. It was phenomenal!

After Chris took the last oxer, Kaya spontaneously applauded, but got an elbow to her ribs from Mrs. Walden. "Hey," she whispered, "don't ruin the price for us. You need to say that the pony is lousy, ugly and probably pumped full of drugs!"

"What?"

"And that you've never met a horse seller you could trust." What did that mean? Horse seller? Weren't they in a training stable? That couldn't be a horse seller.

"I thought..." she began, but then stopped abruptly because Chris was riding over to them.

"Terrific!" she said simply. He looked great. His blond hair stuck wildly out from under his helmet. His shirt was slightly open and his posture was fantastic. He looked like a statue.

"Well, what did you think?" he asked her without saying hi.

"Impressive!" said Kaya and patted the pony's steamy neck. It was clearly in much better shape than

Dreamy, who was as sweaty as a Sumo wrestler after an hour of dressage. On the other hand, Mrs. Walden was right: it was ugly. Nothing about the pony was beautiful. Not the physique, not the head – no, it didn't look at all like a National Championship pony ... more like any old pony from Farmer Smith's or something.

Kaya hid her disappointment. She expected such an expensive pony to be at least as beautiful as Mia's gray pony, if not more beautiful. Gleaming, like Black Beauty, with a symmetrical white star in the middle of its forehead. But this mare was brown. Not chestnut, not bay, just an ordinary brown. The kind of brown that would make a woman run straight to the hairdresser to change the color. She patted the pony's neck again. But what was she supposed to say? Should she lie?

"She jumps like the devil!" Chris beamed at her.

He was right about that. She said, "I've never seen a pony jump like that!"

"If you're up for it, you can ride dressage with her tomorrow. I'd like to watch you then – you notice a lot of different things when you're not on the horse yourself."

"Okay!" She nodded and was happy that he was planning the next day with her. The entire Walden family was watching her with burning eyes – what had she gotten herself into?

A young woman with polished riding boots and a T-shirt with the name of the stable came in and greeted Mr. Walden curtly. She nodded at Kaya and took the pony from Chris. He dismounted; she mounted and rode out on the terrain.

"Now what?" asked Kaya, surprised.

"A quick walk to wind down, to loosen up the joints and muscles. It helps nervous animals get accustomed to environmental noises – they do that here with every horse."

Kaya was impressed. She'd have to tell Claudia about that. This facility was not bad at all.

"You have to tell me a little bit more about Wild Thing," Kaya demanded of Chris. She was curious and if he was talking she wouldn't have to say a thing.

"But first let's get a bite to eat," said Mrs. Walden. "There's a little restaurant here that also happens to be incredibly cheap!" She smiled at her husband.

"Well, I guess we have to cut back somewhere to make up all that money!" He grinned like a wolf in sheep's clothing. "And lately we've been cutting corners on our accommodations, too!"

"Oh Dad, you'll like it. It's really cute!" Chris

nodded to him and Kaya's imagination ran wild: a cute little cabin in the middle of a green meadow. There would be a table in front of it with a red and white checked tablecloth and a bouquet of wildflowers just for them. Inside the cabin, there would be a romantic four-poster bed with a light blue canopy . . . that's where her imagination hit a dead end.

"And when can we take a look at the stables?"

She wanted to know that before joining the Waldens, who were already walking toward the door. Mr. Walden turned around to her smiling. "I think that sometime during the next three days we'll be able to find the time . . ."

He was wearing a soft green cashmere sweater today with light colored slacks, but no blazer. Casual for him, but still, in this environment he looked as if he had just landed from outer space.

Their meal had just been served when Mr. Miller joined them. He was a tall, handsome man with broad shoulders and a narrow waist. He had sparkling blue eyes, a tanned face, and a pleasant smile that inspired confidence – a horseman through and through. Not only that, he was even a state trainer. Kaya looked at him with reverence.

Mr. Walden passed him the menu, but he shook his head and ordered a soda. "This is enough nourishment," he said and Mrs. Walden laughed. She obviously liked wiry Mr. Miller and thought that her husband tended to have a few too many pounds on his frame from too much fine dining.

Kaya looked anxiously over at Chris. Would he start asking Mr. Miller hundreds of questions? No, he was chowing down on the giant pork chop and french fries on his plate. Kaya was hungry, too, but if this conversation had been about *her* brand new pony, she would have set her plate aside ... but since it wasn't about her pony, she started cutting the meat into little pieces. After the first bite she concluded that the food here was pretty good – especially for such low prices. If she told her father about this, he'd probably keel over. In her parents' restaurant, the pork chops cost easily twice as much!

Mr. and Mrs. Walden had both ordered steak, but they were polite enough to talk briefly with Mr. Miller before beginning their meal.

At first Kaya listened with great interest, then out of politeness, but after a while she started daydreaming. After such a big meal she started to feel sleepy. Chris obviously felt the same way and was yawning.

"Can't we go already?" he asked abruptly. The adults had just ordered dessert. This could take a while.

"Kaya's luggage is still in the car," said Mr. Walden. Chris waved his hand and said, "We can easily carry it over. Our cabin isn't very far. I can show Kaya her room and then we can go to bed. It's pretty late already!"

Mrs. Walden checked her watch and was surprised to see that he was right. Mr. Walden accompanied them to the car.

"So, what do you think of Wild Thing?" Chris asked Kaya on the way to the car.

"She's faster, more agile and precise than any big horse," said Kaya spontaneously and wondered how she managed to come up with such a good answer. Mr. Walden nodded. "I'm curious about what will happen tomorrow," he said and handed Chris her suitcase.

So am I, thought Kaya. *But for the time being, I'm curious about what else will happen.*

It had been dark outside for quite a while. Chris walked with her through the night. He had hung her bag loosely over his shoulder as if it weighed nothing, although Kaya was sure that she had stuffed at least 50 pounds' worth of clothes in there. Her

riding boots were still in the car, but Chris carried
everything else on his back. Kaya enjoyed walking
with him through the fields. The footpath was
narrow and led past a few houses, illuminated by the
moon that glowed in the sky like a shiny gold coin.

"Do you believe in the power of the full moon?"
asked Kaya. After five minutes of walking in silence,
she figured one of them had to say something.

"You mean the old stories about witches?"

He looked so good walking next to her. She looked
over at him and found him irresistible. Even the
moonlight looked like it was caught up in his blond
curls. She would've loved to kiss him.

"No, the new ones!"

"The new ones?" He threw her a quizzical glance.
"What are you talking about?"

"Well, that the moonlight influences animals, so
that they become even more active than usual at night.
And people walk in their sleep – or do other things."

Now he seemed to be interested. "What kinds
of things?"

The last house was behind them now and the
footpath seemed to lead to nowhere. At least, it
seemed to pass through the middle of nowhere – in
front of them and on either side there was nothing

but meadow, stretching out to forever. *Not bad*, thought Kaya. She wouldn't have minded spending the night out here with Chris, between the daisies and buttercups. That sounded even more enticing than the cabin with all its rooms. "All kinds," she said and thought hard. What did people do at night, other than sleep? "Some people turn into murderers..."

Oh, that wasn't very smart, she thought. "At least it's supposed to make some people very animated!"

He looked over at her again.

"Do you feel something?" he asked.

"Me???" replied Kaya.

She thought for a minute. *Now or never.*

"Oh, yes!" she said boldly.

"Oh? What?"

Darn. If Alexa were here now, she'd know what to say. What could she be feeling?

"Something tingly. And I'm wide awake – and feeling adventurous!" she replied.

"Me too!"

And he just kept on walking.

But Kaya wasn't ready to give up.

"How do you feel the tingling?" she asked.

"No tingling," he said, totally matter-of-fact, "I'm just feeling adventurous. By the way, do you see that development up ahead? Those are the cabins."

Did he think she was just a little kid? What was up with him? Here they were, walking across fields and meadows by the light of a full moon, and he didn't have a single romantic feeling, not in the slightest! Even though she was just 13, she was way ahead of him, and he was 15 years old!

"Great," said Kaya coolly. Was he still thinking about her older sister? Kaya had more things in her head than this 15-year-old boy. Maybe she needed to make this clear to him again.

He switched her bag to his other shoulder.

"You'll see. The cabin is totally cool. Our rooms are next to each other, but that shouldn't be a problem for you since I don't snore."

He laughed at his own joke and Kaya gave him a dirty look. Was he nuts?

"My father was pretty annoyed, because he usually stays in hotels with all the extras, but a little country air will do him good!"

Kaya bit her lip. One could only hope that the country air would benefit his wife, too.

"See over there?" Chris pointed ahead. "There, between the trees, that one's ours. It's the one way on the right skirting the big meadow. If we feel like it, we can bring Wild Thing back here and let him graze on it."

"Don't they have any paddocks here?"

"Probably, but not for the training horses."

"Poor things."

Chris didn't say anything, just stopped suddenly.

"What is it?" asked Kaya, startled.

He dropped her suitcase and started digging around in his pockets.

"Come on, tell me what's wrong!"

"Can you remember if my mother gave me the key to the cabin?"

She couldn't remember. Both parents had said goodnight to her in the restaurant, then Mr. Walden walked them over to the car, got out her suitcase and locked the car again.

"Not in my presence."

She looked at Chris. He had changed his clothes back at the stable, and was now wearing jeans, a gray polo shirt and sneakers. There weren't many places the keys could be.

"Check one more time," she said.

He patted his pockets and checked in all of them one more time. Then he shook his head and cursed. "This just can't be!"

No, thought Kaya, *it really can't.*

"Drat! Now I'll have to go back!"

"Should I take a look?"

"Thanks, but there's no need, I'm familiar enough with my pockets myself." He took a deep breath. "You can take your bag and walk to the house. There's a bench in front – make yourself comfortable."

"And you?" asked Kaya meekly, because the thought of sitting out there all alone in the dark scared her to pieces.

"I'll run back quickly!"

Quickly? To the restaurant and back would take at least a half hour if not 40 minutes!

"I'll come along!" she said decisively. Farewell, dream of exploring the cabin without any interruption. His parents would surely return with them then.

"Wait a minute!" she said and instinctively reached for his hand. "What about open windows? Or maybe there's a key under the mat or something?"

Not only did he leave her hand where it was, he squeezed it, too. "Hey, you are terrific! That's right. I'm an idiot. My mom put the keys in the flowerpot in case my father missed us!" Now he laughed.

"What luck! I would've walked back there like a dummy and my mother would have treated me like one!" He hugged Kaya and gave her a kiss on her forehead. "Thanks for the damage control!"

"The what?"

"Oh nothing, my mother always says stuff like that. She's a lawyer, you know. I was just trying to say that you saved me from embarrassing myself."

They stood facing each other. Chris's arms were on Kaya's shoulders, and their faces were close together. Except for the nighttime noises from the nearby forest, it was completely quiet. Neither of them moved and suddenly Kaya felt Chris's lips brush her own. She hardly dared to breathe so as not to scare him off. Otherwise he might snap out of it and see that she was in front of him and not Alexa or someone else!

She tried to think about what she was supposed to do next. But then she just closed her eyes and quickly kissed him back. It just happened the way it happens. And then, although it was out of place, she started to think about those old movies and the romantic scenes between Cary Grant and Audrey Hepburn – or whoever. Didn't all of them close their eyes when they kissed? Since it was her first kiss, she wanted to enjoy the scene. She was just wondering what would happen next when they heard a car. Shortly thereafter, headlights shone through the trees, and since the footpath and the road ran parallel to each other leading up to the cabins, it was obvious that in a few seconds they would be in the spotlight. *Darn!* thought Kaya.

Chris let go of her and looked at her. "You're a good kisser," he said in such a surprised tone of voice that suggested that he hadn't expected that at all.

"Oh, I do it every day," she said with such earnestness that she hardly believed herself.

"Aha!" he said and then hoisted her bag back on his shoulder. "Well, let's head up to the house."

Kaya nodded obediently, although he couldn't see that, and trotted half next to and half behind him because now Chris and his long legs were suddenly moving a lot faster than hers.

The car came closer and bathed them in bright light before driving on. Kaya couldn't make out a thing, but found it strange that the Waldens didn't stop.

"Those are our neighbors," explained Chris quickly. "I would have known that if I had listened more closely," he said.

"Why's that?"

"Because we don't have a diesel!"

The cabin really was quite cute. It stood away from the other cabins, and after Chris unlocked the door and turned on the outside lights, Kaya saw that it stood in the middle of a meadow full of wildflowers.

"This is cool!" she said. "I've been wanting to turn our backyard into a meadow full of wildflowers like this, but my parents are too boring. They always want the lawn mowed, yuck!"

Chris nodded silently and waved for her to come in. What was he thinking now? wondered Kaya . . . was he going to kiss her again? She would have liked that but at the same time she felt strangely inhibited, which just made her mad. It was ridiculous, really – you were constantly reading about the girl taking the initiative. Girls' magazines were full of stories like that, but when it came right down to it, the girl still waited for the boy to take the first step.

Kaya, she thought to herself, *you will now walk straight over to him, put your arms around his neck and kiss him.*

But Chris had already walked away.

"So, this is the living room," he explained to her what she could already see for herself, "with an attached kitchen. Up front are both of our rooms, the bathroom is across from them and all the way in the back is my parents' bedroom."

Kaya looked down the hall wordlessly. She couldn't imagine meeting Mr. Walden in the morning on the way to the bathroom. No wonder he was annoyed. No doubt he was used to always having his own bathroom.

Chris carried her luggage into her room and she followed him. On the outside, the house looked like a log cabin, but here on the inside the walls were whitewashed. It was charming, even though it was a little small. A bed, a closet, a small table and a floor lamp – there wasn't enough space for more than that. But the bedspread and upholstery were done in friendly fabrics that made the room look downright cozy. She could stand living here.

"And you?" she asked.

Chris motioned to the wall that separated the two rooms. "Same thing, just different colors. Less orange and yellow, more blue and green."

The boy's room, in other words. A boy and a girl, the traditional nuclear family. Kaya smiled.

"Now what?" she asked.

"Now we go to bed!" he answered. That wasn't what she had hoped to hear.

"Are you tired?" she asked.

"I'm wiped out after today," he said and began yawning, as if on cue.

"Despite the full moon?"

"Tomorrow is another day!"

One day was already over, thought Kaya, but an uninterrupted night? Maybe they could send Chris's parents to dinner alone tomorrow.

"Tomorrow my mother plans to cook for us here, so prepare for the worst."

She should have expected that. The total family experience. So that kiss would be a one-time thing, never to happen again. She was disappointed when he raised his hand to wave goodnight to her, like Sitting Bull or something. He walked toward the door, but then he stopped at the threshold and turned around one more time. "Do you really kiss every day?" he asked.

His eyebrows were pulled together and he was bent forward slightly in anticipation of her answer.

"Of course," she said offhandedly. What was she supposed to say to a question like that? No, you were my first kiss? She couldn't possibly ever admit that. It would be too babyish.

"Okay then," he said, "good night," and walked out, pulling the door shut behind him.

Kaya looked at the door in disbelief and sank down on the bed, disappointed. Was she supposed to understand what had just happened? No, she didn't have to. But now she understood her mother. She frequently threw up her hands and said, "Just try to understand men!" Today Kaya got her first inkling of what her mother meant by that.

There was a loud knock. Kaya needed a few seconds to realize that the knock was at her own door. She opened her eyes and slowly remembered where she was, but she still felt like she was dreaming. Sunlight poured through the open curtains and flooded the room with light. A rag rug lay on the floor in front of her bed. On the wall behind her head was a picture of a horse; a galloping horse on a paddock, which they didn't have here, if Chris was right.

Chris.

Slowly she remembered what had happened the night before. Her eyes fell on her suitcase on the floor next to her bed. She had been too tired last night and didn't have the energy to unpack. Now, some of her stuff was on the floor, some was on the table and the rest just hung out of her bag.

Suddenly she felt sad. He had simply gone last night. Goodnight and good-bye. Was that the way it was supposed to happen? She felt so alone. And she was, too. After such a promising beginning in the woods, he just went straight to bed last night. Tired as an old man. Suddenly she felt outraged. Or was she sad? She wasn't too clear about her own feelings, but then there was another knock on her door, this time a little louder. Then she heard a voice, "Kaya, wake up, breakfast is ready!"

That was Mrs. Walden. She'd have to be good. "Okay, thank you, I'll be right there!" she called out in a happy tone of voice. Kaya looked at her watch: 7 am. Unbelievable. Who willingly got up at seven in the morning on vacation? But then she remembered that she was supposed to ride Wild Thing today and her heart skipped a beat. A National Championship pony! Suddenly she was wide-awake and raring to go.

Hopefully it would go well.

Still, she knew that Dreamy was a better fit for her than this brown mare, even if she was an incredible jumper.

"If you're not good looking, then you have to be hard working." Why did she suddenly think of this horrible pronouncement that Alexa angrily brought home from school one day? The whole family had debated it over dinner. Her father felt that it had an element of truth in it, but her mother found it infuriating.

"Am I good looking?" she asked her husband, who quickly said yes.

"And am I hard working?" she asked next. After he again said yes, Kaya's mother concluded that the prejudice was now proven to be completely false.

Still, Kaya couldn't get it out of her head. Maybe the cutest foals were spoiled quickly and the ugly ones failed to get any attention until they realized that they had to fight to be noticed. She sat on her bed, lost in thought, when there was another knock at the door. This time it was Chris. "The bathroom is free."

Mrs. Walden had set the breakfast table. It was strange to be suddenly sitting at a table with a whole new family as if it were the most normal thing in the world. Today Mr. Walden was wearing a checked shirt and dark blue linen trousers. This was probably the most casual outfit his closet offered. Kaya found that thought amusing.

When she compared him to her father, who wore a suit on the rarest occasions – only for big celebrations and only if her mother insisted – but usually walked around in jeans and T-shirts, well,

Mr. Walden was a lot more formal. He even ate his toast with a fork and knife! Mrs. Walden, on the other hand, had a bowl of cereal with yogurt and sliced fruit.

"Well?" she asked Kaya as she came out of the bathroom, "would you like a little energy boost?"

She could definitely use a little energy, but she wanted to first wait and see what Chris would be eating. He shoved a slice of toast with honey into his mouth in the same way that she did at home. That was a relief . . . now she didn't have to pretend.

Mrs. Walden had bought the previously mentioned cereal and yoghurt and a jar of honey, as well as milk and a loaf of bread, so there was plenty to choose from. They sat around the table for more than half an hour, but then Chris became impatient and got up.

"I think it's time we got going!" He looked over at Kaya and she felt herself blushing. Oh no, not that! She had to come up with some excuse for the silly redness in her face. "I'm really excited!" she said quickly. "Never in a million years would I have dreamed that I'd get to ride a National Championship pony!"

Mr. Walden gave her an understanding nod. "You'll do fine," he said. She liked that. Whenever someone said 'you'll do fine' to you, it was because they had so much faith in you that it was practically a self-fulfilling prophecy. Good. She'd do fine.

"Did we make an appointment yesterday? Is Mr. Miller waiting for us?" She looked at Chris again but didn't blush because she was already bright red. The way he kissed her yesterday and the way he looked today ... his hair was still damp from the shower and the turquoise polo shirt looked so perfect on his tan skin. His jeans hung easily on his hips and he wore a wide casual leather belt with them that made him look even cuter. Boy, was she hooked on him. But the way he said good morning was so cool and business-like that she only gave him a vague smile. That was the worst: acting one way when you felt a totally different way.

She sighed.

"Now, now," said Mrs. Walden and smiled at her. "It won't be that bad!"

Oh it's bad enough, she thought. But then she smiled and said, "No, just the opposite. I'm really looking forward to it!"

"Okay, folks, then let's start clearing the table!"

For Chris, it looked like clearing the table was totally a matter of course. He stacked the dirty plates, carried them into the kitchen and put them all right into the dishwasher. Kaya helped Mrs. Walden put away the breakfast food while Mr. Walden stayed in his seat.

"My husband," said Mrs. Walden frostily. "His mother spoiled him rotten, and to this day he hasn't learned that other women don't necessarily think that way!"

"Maybe he doesn't want to learn," said Kaya quietly. "My father likes to duck out when it comes to this sort of work too, but my mother always finds him in one of his favorite play areas."

"Play areas?" asked Mrs. Walden, bemused.

"Sure. In front of the computer, behind the newspaper, under the car . . ."

Mrs. Walden laughed heartily. "Sounds like you have a fun household."

Kaya thought for a minute. "Yes, I suppose we do. We laugh a lot, even though my parents are always working very hard. I think they need it for balance."

"That's a very wise observation, Kaya. Even though you're just thirteen."

"Already thirteen!" Kaya corrected her and then licked the honey off her finger that got stuck there as she closed the jar.

"Well, are you ready?" Chris stood in the doorway.

"My son will be a good one, too," said Mrs. Walden.

He already is, thought Kaya. Chris raised his eyebrows at the same time. "Mo-om!" he said, drawing it out into two syllables, the same way she did when she found something was unbearably embarrassing. And mothers could be terribly embarrassing. Strange that they themselves never seemed to notice.

"I'm ready!" said Kaya, trying to change the subject. She was wearing a light blue blouse and light blue and gray checkered riding pants. In addition, and considering the circumstances, she had pulled her hair back in a bun. She looked good – at least that's what she concluded after checking herself out in the bathroom mirror. Hopefully he thought so, too.

"Sounds good," he nodded at her. "Do we have any carrots?" he asked his mother, who motioned to a small cabinet.

"Plenty!"

Mr. Walden was still sitting at the table. His eyes were closed and he was clearly relaxed.

"Do you even want to come?" asked his wife.

He opened his eyes. "What kind of a question is that? Wasn't this whole thing my idea?"

Not Chris?

Now Kaya was totally disappointed. Hadn't Mr.

Walden said to her that Chris told him about her skill in dressage? Should she ask him about that? But she decided to let it go.

They got into the back of Mrs. Walden's jeep. It was definitely not an inexpensive car ... having money could be a very pleasant thing, thought Kaya, and she understood why her sister wanted to earn a lot. That was the lesson she learned after spending a year among wealthy people. If you don't have much yourself, then you constantly have to figure out where you can participate and then be extremely grateful for every chance. She secretly promised herself to try harder in school. After all, she wanted to have her own horse someday, and a jeep and a horse transporter. She smiled dreamily out the window as Mrs. Walden turned the car around. She'd need a horseman, too. Chris. Then they could put their money together and they'd have a lovely life. She looked into his eyes, but he just grinned at her.

Then he moved his hand away and stretched out on his side of the car.

"I think it's really cool that you came along and are doing this for me!" he said. Loud and clear. His father turned around and nodded to him. "Yes, I watched her ride Dreamy the other day – she was great. I'd never seen him like that before!"

That's because you were never in the stable before, thought Kaya, although she had to agree with him. That had really been a masterful performance, although she still didn't know what inspired it. Maybe Dreamy wanted to switch from being a jumper to a dressage pony? But that was ridiculous; he got bored silly with all that.

They drove back the same way Chris and Kaya had walked last night. There, there was the spot where they had kissed. She looked over to him, but Chris didn't show any reaction. *Just wait,* she thought. *If you're looking for a challenge, then you can have one.* After all, they had two more days.

"We're almost there," said Mrs. Walden cheerfully. Once again she looked like she could be one of the riding stable personnel. A simple T-shirt and faded jeans. The total opposite of her husband.

"I'm quite excited," Mr. Walden said.

"How do you think I feel!" said Chris, winking at Kaya. His mistake was that he was treating her like a little sister again. *I'm going to ride his mare so well, that he'll have no choice but to fall in love with me,* thought Kaya. After making her resolution, she got out.

Wild Thing was already groomed and tacked, standing outside of his stall.

"That's a shame, really," said Kaya. "I find that you really get to know a horse if you do it all yourself." She pulled out a carrot and gave it to Wild Thing. As the mare munched her snack, Kaya stroked her enormous nose, thinking that her head was clearly too big. But then again, Kaya had a big nose, too. Neither of them could help that.

"Okay," said Kaya and looked around. "Where do they keep the saddles?" Chris went with her, and shortly thereafter Kaya led Wild Thing into the arena. "Coming through!" she called out, even though she was the only one there. That was a good thing; this way no one would get in her way. On the other hand, it was a real drawback that she couldn't observe how Wild Thing interacted with other horses. On the jumping course yesterday there weren't any other horses either.

"We're going to go to the office and have some coffee," announced Mrs. Walden. That was fine with Kaya.

At least the mare wasn't saddle shy. Kaya carefully tightened the girth and Chris held the stirrup down on the other side until she had mounted.

"Is there anything in particular that I should know?" she asked.

"No, just the usual. First a good walk to warm her up and loosen her joints. Nothing special."

"No problem." Kaya nodded at him. "And what'll you give me if she gives a super performance?" That slipped out before she realized what she was saying.

"What do you want?" he squinted at her inquiringly.

She knew exactly what she wanted, but she couldn't say it to him.

"Why don't you think of something appropriate?" she said.

"And what if you ride really badly, lose control or even get thrown? Well, what then?"

"Then you get to wish for something!"

He nodded. "It's a deal!"

"Do you know what you want?" she asked quickly.

"I'll let you know when the time comes!"

She struck off and he waved to her as he left the arena. Darn, he was outsmarting her today. 'I'll let you know when the time comes' – that's what she should have said. She walked for over ten minutes.

She didn't want to risk any injury. Horse tendons were extremely sensitive, and she didn't want to make the horse lame. Then she took up the reins and began to trot. The mare had a supple back and felt soft, pleasant. She had a broad walk, but her trot was that of a larger horse. Where did this pony get that from? The mare was truly a hard worker, Kaya noticed immediately. Her impulsion was tremendous – it was so great that Kaya had to slow her down. Good thing the hall was so large. Back home she would have nicked the edges like a trotter. Kaya shortened the reins and rode serpentines through the arena and was utterly charmed. Sitting on Wild Thing made you feel like you were on the most beautiful pony around. She was incredibly responsive. Even in a sitting trot, Wild Thing was a dream. All you had to do was think the cues for a gallop and she obeyed. Kaya was absolutely thrilled, so she stopped in front of the window to the office and gave the thumbs up. From farther away the pane was reflective, but from closer up Kaya could see that by now Mr. Miller was there too. The adults sat around a large table drinking coffee and waved to her. She figured that what she was doing out here looked good from in there, too. Then she got a little more adventuresome and began with some more difficult exercises. But the mare continued to prove herself to be elastic. At a strong trot, Kaya felt like she was gliding through clouds. Wild Thing's length of stride was indescribable.

"Hey, I thought you were a jumper," she said to the mare as she loosened the reins and began to thank her and stroke her for such an excellent hour of riding. Chris walked into the arena.

"What do you think?" he asked.

"Fantastic!" said Kaya, out of breath. "I'm in love. She is indescribable. She moves like a big horse, with pure, even rhythms. It's just incredible. I don't have enough experience to evaluate everything, but I do have a fabulous feeling!"

"You looked great together, too!" He nodded enthusiastically and patted Wild Thing's neck.

"If you can hold on for a minute, I'll saddle up another pony that's up for sale, and then we can go out together for an hour and a half or so. It's Mr. Miller's idea."

"That's really nice of him!"

"Yeah, he seems like a great guy."

Kaya and Chris walked outside with the ponies, even ventured a gallop on a small hill, but Kaya felt that

Wild Thing had done enough work already. They continued on at a leisurely pace and before they knew it, they wound up in front of the cabin.

"Well, well," said Chris, "how convenient! Let's take out their bits and then they can graze a little while we get a drink. My rear end is starting to ache in these jeans!"

The key was back in the flowerpot. Chris brought out two glasses of lemonade.

"Now you have to say what you want," he said and gave Kaya her drink.

She put her glass down on the table, loosened Wild Thing's girth and took out her bit. Then she pulled the reins over her head and held them as she watched him go for the juiciest tufts of grass.

"Well?" asked Chris, who stood next to her with Laszlo, a sleek black pony.

"I'm still thinking," said Kaya.

It was just beautiful here. Lush green everywhere plus all those fruit trees, the rolling meadows, the colorful flowers, the butterflies and the cozy cabin with the wood table and benches. She would love to stay here longer with him.

"It's so beautiful here!" she said. "I wish I could stay here for two weeks!"

At first he didn't say anything. But then he shook his head.

"I was hoping you'd ask for something easier, like maybe a kiss. But that . . ."

Kaya had to laugh. "Oh, a kiss will do, too,"

And then, standing out on the meadow next to their ponies, they kissed briefly, because Laszlo suddenly took a leap, ripping the reins out of Chris's hands and stopped a few feet away from them. Wild Thing noticed what he did, but didn't follow suit. Kaya immediately recognized the problem. A huge horsefly had set itself down on Laszlo's back. That explained the pony's panicked reaction. But now they had a problem.

Kaya shooed the insect and Chris was irritated.

"Darn!" he said, but Kaya calmed him down.

"Don't worry. We'll get him. Do you have something in your pocket for him?"

Chris patted down his jeans, then shook his head.

"Okay, hold on." She passed Wild Thing's reins to him and slowly approached Laszlo. The black pony stood as still as a statue. He held his Thoroughbred head high, his mane erect. The reins swung loosely. The pony was ready to bolt.

This was the worst possible situation. The busy

road passed right between the cabin and the riding hall and they had no way of knowing how familiar the pony was with the facility. Maybe it would try to run to its home stable? They just had to catch him!

"Ho, ho," said Kaya. "Staaaaaay, fella, staaaay. Ho, ho." She spoke quietly and reassuringly and she walked over to him slowly with her hand outstretched.

He looked her over, but did not relax in the least.

"Nothing's going to happen to you," she said again. "Ho, hooooo."

Kaya had almost reached him, but the expression in his eyes worried her. Pure fear. How could a pony be so frightened? She stopped. Maybe he would take the decisive step toward her. She continued to hold her hand out to him when she suddenly heard Chris behind her.

"No," she said, but it was too late. Laszlo suddenly broke away.

He ran so fast that the reins flew nearly straight in the air and he bucked and kicked at the same time.

"If we were on the paddock, I'd enjoy this," said Chris, pressing his lips together, "but here? Should I follow him on Wild Thing? Maybe he'll come to her."

"Aargh," Kaya groaned. If Chris hadn't been so

hasty, they wouldn't have this problem, but it was no use thinking about that now.

"Try it," she said, and tightened the girth while Chris took up the reins. This mare was truly a wonder. She looked over at Laszlo, but didn't show the least desire to follow him in his break for freedom. Chris mounted quickly and all Kaya could think to do was to call after him, "careful with her legs!" and suddenly felt like her own mother.

Chris galloped off and Kaya followed him with her eyes. Before long, Laszlo was little more than a black dot, trotting way up ahead near the hills. Wild Thing followed, galloping like a rocket.

Kaya walked over to the wooden table and sat down on the bench. A kiss and its consequences, she thought. She'd probably never forget it. Yesterday Chris broke off because a car was coming and today because a pony bolted. At this rate they'd never get anywhere. She picked up her lemonade and downed it in one gulp. Maybe the liquid would help clear her head. She certainly needed all her senses. Should she call Mrs. Walden? But she didn't have her cell phone number. And she didn't have Mr. Walden's cell phone number either; just their home phone and

Charlotte's cell phone. But she definitely didn't feel like including her in this adventure just yet.

Should she call the office at the riding arena? If she did, she'd probably get Mr. Miller on the phone. But if Chris had already captured Laszlo, then she would worry everyone needlessly . . . and would have to pay the consequences.

Kaya downed the second glass of lemonade. She just didn't know what to do! And sitting there doing nothing was the worst. If only there were a bicycle around. Then she could catch up to Chris and the ponies. But on foot?

There was no sign of Laszlo anymore and she could just make out Wild Thing over by the hill. Besides, they weren't even running toward the stable! The stable was in the opposite direction. Or was she mistaken?

She paced back and forth a few more times and then decided to inform Mr. Miller. If something really bad were to happen then it would be unforgivable not to have called for help. Inside the cabin she looked around for the phone book. She found a ratty copy inside a desk drawer. Four years old. She figured the training center must have been around back then and paged through the directory. But what should she look under? She didn't know the exact name of the stable and wasn't sure of the address, either. Riding Hall? Horse Center? Training Center? Maybe the family name? And what was the name of the village it was in?

She took the phone book outside with her. There was no sign of Chris anywhere. Now it was getting serious. She had just decided to dial 911 when her cell phone rang. It was Chris. He had her phone number.

"I've got him," he said, and sounded out of breath.

"Thank goodness!" Kaya exhaled loudly. He was a real hero.

"And did anything happen to him?"

"Just a torn rein, nothing more. Listen, I'm on my way back with both of them, but you have to stall my mother. She just called me because she wants to pick us up at the stable to go to lunch."

"Uh-oh. And you didn't tell her a thing?"

"Of course not. I don't need another problem!"

What luck that she didn't have his mother's cell phone number, thought Kaya. Otherwise they'd be in a mess now. "What do we do?"

"I told her that I went galloping with Laszlo and that you were going easy on Wild Thing, walking slowly behind us. She thought that was very responsible of you."

Now she had points for being responsible. Not bad!

"And what should I say to her?"

"No idea. Just play for time. Lock up the cabin and put the key back in the flowerpot. Then get out of there and come meet up with me because she should be at the cabin any minute now!"

Kaya looked frantically over at the road. If she was supposed to be riding slowly over to the stable, then it wouldn't be wise to get caught here.

And that was just dandy. This guy came up with a really great idea ... now she had to go running clear across the field, in her riding boots but without a pony, like a fool. And she had to be careful not to let anyone see her, or their story would be exposed.

She ran off immediately. At about the same time, she noticed that her riding boots were too tight. The fact that there were tons of holes in the field didn't make it any easier.

When she suddenly heard a car, she dashed behind a tree to hide. She felt like she had already gone a good distance, but she was still visible from the house. Indeed, she had no trouble at all recognizing that it was Mrs. Walden who got out of the jeep. Good thing that she didn't have a dog with her, or it would be yapping, running off to greet Kaya.

She waited until Chris's mother disappeared into the house and wanted to continue onward when the cell phone rang. In the display it said Unknown Caller, but Kaya was sure that it had to be Mrs. Walden. She started rhythmically bouncing against the tree trunk, hoping that it sounded like she was on a horse and answered the phone.

"Oh Kaya, thanks for answering so quickly!"

Did she answer too quickly? For someone riding a horse, she did. How thoughtless.

"It's Simone Walden."

Aha, Simone!

"Yes, hello!"

She felt pretty foolish, rubbing against the apple tree and hoping it sounded like the real thing.

"Chris already told me that you took a different route, but I think he said you'd both be back at the stable soon. I reserved a table for us all in the restaurant we went to yesterday. Fred is with Mr. Miller right now, bargaining over the price and then we'll hopefully have something to celebrate!"

Kaya forgot about the tree.

"Really?"

She sounded so surprised that Simone had to laugh.

"Yes, really! Both of you rode her so convincingly that we can drive back home again today!"

Oh no! Kaya couldn't hide her disappointment and had to lean against the tree for support. This was just awful. If only she hadn't ridden so well. Why had she tried so hard? She ruined everything! No more evening with Chris, not a single one! She could have burst into tears right then and there!

"Aren't you happy?"

She must have noticed how quiet Kaya was. Kaya started to rub against the tree again.

"Oh yes, I'm happy for Chris," she said honestly, "but not for myself . . ." and added quickly, "it's just so beautiful out here!"

At first it was silent on the other end.

"Ah well," she heard Mrs. Walden say. "I could talk to Fred again. Maybe he can handle staying here another day!"

"All right!" said Kaya quickly. "That'd be wonderful. Besides, you were going to cook dinner tonight . . . I was looking forward to that!"

She thought about what Chris had said about his mother's cooking skills, but it didn't matter anymore. Even if they were going to have fried ants, at least they'd be sitting together and having another evening for themselves.

She heard Mrs. Walden laugh again brightly. "Normally nobody is very happy when I cook!"

"Oh I've heard otherwise," Kaya fibbed. "Besides, I could help you!"

"Okay, okay, I'll see what I can do, but first we'll meet up at the stable in half an hour. Is it a deal?"

Kaya looked past her tree to the house. Mrs. Walden was probably standing at the window with her phone. They could wave to each other.

"It's a deal," she said and put her phone away.

A deal? In half an hour?? How was she supposed to manage that? She looked up ahead to the hill that Chris disappeared behind. It would take her at least half an hour to get over there – and how could she even know how much farther he had ridden from there?

Kaya looked back at the house again and when it looked like the coast was clear, she started running again. Who'd be interested in a lonely rider running across the field without her horse?

By the time she finally spotted Chris, her feet felt like they were on fire. He rode over leisurely, leading Laszlo over the knoll.

"There you are finally!" he called to her. "I was afraid I'd have to go back alone!"

Kaya couldn't think of a good comeback to that. She was sweating and every step hurt. She was at the end of her rope and he had the nerve to say something like that.

"Now hold on!" she said lamely and stopped in her tracks until Chris reached her. She took Laszlo's reins from him and saw that his coat looked shaggy with perspiration. He had to be dripping wet.

"If we bring him back looking like this, then it will be obvious that he took off on an unplanned steeplechase!"

She observed Wild Thing, whose ears twitched adventurously. Galloping around didn't seem to have been particularly strenuous for her; at least her coat wasn't covered with drying sweat.

Chris knew what to do. "I'll take him straight to the wash stall. And you distract everyone with Wild Thing."

He jumped down from his mare and mounted the black pony. He didn't seem all that happy about it, because the little runaway was clearly tired.

Kaya shimmied onto Wild Thing and adjusted the stirrups, which were much too long now.

"Your mother is expecting to meet us at the stable in a few minutes."

Chris gave her a crooked smile and Kaya thought he was irresistible, even though she had just been plenty annoyed with him.

"My mother doesn't have much of a sense of time. It drives my father nuts. And unfortunately, that's something I inherited from him!" He gave her another impish grin and rode off. *Good golly*, thought Kaya.

By the time they reached the stable, Chris had told her the entire story. A small ditch filled with water had finally stopped Laszlo. He paced up and down alongside it, agitated, but didn't dare to jump over it. The water in it gurgled loudly, but it was half covered by plants, and that seemed so eerie to Laszlo that when Wild Thing approached, he turned around and looked at her longingly.

"He was downright grateful!" laughed Chris. "But I had to be careful that Wild Thing didn't just jump over the ditch herself – she was really getting into it!"

They both laughed and Kaya patted the mare's neck.

"Yesiree, she is truly splendid!" she laughed. "Did you know that your father is buying her right now?"

He seemed surprised.

"Is he really?"

"Your mother told me when she called!"

He nodded. "Yes, sometimes they are totally cool!"

Totally cool, sure, you could call them that. If parents could fork over as much as a hundred thousand dollars for a pony of this caliber, then that certainly was totally cool. She should teach her parents how to be totally cool. She had to laugh.

"What is it?" he asked.

"Isn't Laszlo listed for sale as a jumper? Someone's not going to be very happy!"

Chris laughed with her. "Well, at least he's gorgeous. Maybe that's enough for the new owner."

Mrs. Walden stood outside the riding hall and made a point of looking at her watch.

"Okay, okay," called Chris. "It's my fault!"

His mother walked over to him and when she got a closer look at Laszlo, she gave her son an inquisitive look.

"Did he bolt?" she asked.

"You could call it that," nodded Chris. "He's pretty hot-tempered."

Simone looked at Kaya. "And you look pretty disheveled, too."

"Dishev ... what?"

"A bit mussed up, you're a bit of a mess," said Chris, smiling and explained what had happened to his mother, who was walking between them. "That wasn't my fault, though, she did that herself!"

Yes, too bad, Kaya said to herself silently. As she dismounted, she couldn't help yelping in pain.

"Are you okay?" asked Simone Walden immediately. "Is something hurting you?

Kaya could barely stand. Her feet hurt so much that she felt tears shoot into her eyes. "My boots have gotten too small for me," she said quietly and limped next to the mare into the stable. Wild Thing nudged her, looking for a snack, but Kaya had nothing left. "I'll bring you something in a sec," she promised, "besides, today is your lucky day!"

A groom took the mare from her, which was fine with Kaya, who sank down on the nearest bench.

"Boots don't get too tight over night! You need new riding boots!"

Simone stood next to her and held a bootjack in her hand.

"Off with them!" she said, and took the matter into her own hands, much to Kaya's dismay. Suddenly out popped her aching feet in her threadbare socks through which fat, blood-red blisters shimmered.

"Oh, good heavens!" Mrs. Walden was truly shocked. "First I'll prepare a footbath for you. And you can't put on those boots again; they'll torture your feet. You need new ones!"

Kaya didn't say a word. New leather riding boots were sinfully expensive, $180 at least. She had been thrilled to pieces when she got this pair, which she bought used, because before that, she wore rubber boots. How could she explain to a woman who thought nothing of buying a National Championship pony that her parents simply didn't have any money left over for simple riding boots?

Chris came over to the two of them, took one look at her feet and furrowed his brow. "Did you jog next to Wild Thing the whole time instead of riding her?" Then he gave her that naughty grin of his and Kaya threw the first thing she got her hands on at him – a hard piece of horse dung.

"Ouch!" he said and Simone Walden had to laugh. "You deserved that. And now tell me how we're going to get her over to the jeep without any shoes?"

"A wheelchair?" he asked and rubbed his head.

"You're big and strong and she's small and delicate. What do you think?"

"That she needs to grow?"

Simone Walden shook her head slowly, and that's how Chris wound up carrying Kaya to the car. Kaya thought she was dreaming and she suddenly thought of the story her father told her about carrying her mother as a young bride over the threshold of their apartment. Only he tripped and crashed into the coat stand and they were buried under all their coats and jackets. Wasn't that romantic!

Think about something else, she told herself, but by then they had reached the car. Chris let her slide gently into her seat. That almost felt nicer than being carried. Now she could have wrapped her arms around him and kissed him, but Simone Walden was holding the car door open and decided that she should sit in the back and put her legs up across the seat. "First we'll stop at the pharmacy and then we'll go to the restaurant. Fred will drive over with Mr. Miller, but that's sure to take a while, knowing my husband."

Chris got into the front passenger's seat and waited for his mother to start the car.

"What are they doing, anyway?" he asked his mother, acting innocent.

"I'd say they're bargaining."

He saw Kaya's face in the rear view mirror. She was smiling mischievously, like a little girl. Now she was waiting for Chris's reaction, and he was playing the surprised, but elated son. "Really? So quickly?" He put his arm on his mother's shoulder and gave her a loud kiss on her cheek. Simone laughed. "Yes, but first she needs a thorough inspection. We don't buy anything blind!"

"Inspection?" Kaya had never heard of anything like that.

"A veterinarian will give her a complete check-up to see if she's healthy, then he'll examine her tendons, x-ray her bones and so on."

Chris turned around to look at her. His eyes were sparkling more than usual.

"And if she's okay, then we'll be off!" He winked at Kaya and then hugged his mother again until she said, "Stop! Stop!" because she had just turned onto a country road.

Did he say 'we'? Was he talking about himself and Kaya? Or himself and Wild Thing?

"But please don't get too excited yet," warned his mother. "Your father is still negotiating, and you know he can be a tough customer!"

72

"But once he knows he wants something, then he does some serious bargaining, and it sounds like he's made up his mind!"

Simone nodded.

"You two also did a terrific job. Like pros. Even Mr. Miller was impressed."

Kaya felt herself go red again; she felt the color creep up her neck and into her cheeks. She had been praised by Mr. Miller – by a state trainer! Now if that didn't mean something!

The only thing nicer would have been a kiss from Chris.

They were on their second glass of lemonade when Mr. Walden finally arrived, but without Mr. Miller. Both agreed that the pony was made for Chris, but they couldn't agree on the price, explained Chris's father.

"He wants to ask the owner one more time, but doesn't think that he'll accept my last offer."

"What was your last offer?" asked Chris, whose face was colored by disappointment.

"He wants seventy thousand and I offered sixty thousand as well as the cost of a full examination."

"That's surely enough," said Kaya impulsively.

"But Dad, because of just ten?" groaned Chris.

Mrs. Walden remained calm and shrugged her shoulders. "Let's just wait and see what happens. When does he plan to get back to you?"

Kaya looked involuntarily over at Chris. Her heart was racing again from all this excitement and she wondered how he was feeling now.

"As soon as he's talked it over with the current owner."

"Can't we do that ourselves?"

"No, they want the sale to be handled by Mr. Miller and to not have anything to do with it themselves." Mr. Walden took a deep breath. "That's something we'll have to accept and just be patient with, although that doesn't mean that we won't head home today."

"Oh no!" that slipped out of Kaya's mouth again and she quickly put her hand over her mouth.

"Oh no?" asked Mr. Walden, surprised. "What else do we want to do here? We've done as much as we can for now. Everything else will run its course, and if we're to get Wild Thing, then we'll hire a horse specialist to look her over. Why should we hang out here doing nothing?"

Everyone was looking at her, even Chris.

"But it's so beautiful here," said Kaya quietly and

didn't know where she should look. "And I was having such a nice time."

Everyone was quiet. Kaya saw Mrs. Walden give her husband a nudge under the table. She had no idea what that was supposed to mean, but Mr. Walden dropped the subject and called over the waiter to order lunch.

It was early afternoon by the time they got back to
their cabin and black clouds pulled in over the hill
Laszlo and Wild Thing had run over that morning. It
was clear that the adults wanted to be alone, so Chris
and Kaya tried to come up with something to do.

"It doesn't look like going swimming is a good
idea," he said, pointing to the dark clouds that were
blowing in on a strong gust of wind. Kaya sensed that
the first heavy drops would start falling any minute
now and then there'd be a huge downpour. Still, she
said, "wet is wet!"

Chris laughed.

"We could just stand outside with our arms
outstretched. That'd have the same effect!"

Kaya thought the idea wasn't bad. They could
stretch their arms out and run to each other in slow
motion like a cheesy movie, but she was pretty sure

that wasn't what Chris had in mind. He just wanted to go outside, stretch out his arms, and get wet.

"We could play a game," she suggested.

"A game?" The bored way he said that word made it clear what he thought of her idea. Baby stuff.

"A computer game!" she said quickly.

"You mean you think they have an Internet cafe in this hick town?" He sounded more interested, but still he frowned. "You don't really believe that, do you?"

No, she didn't.

"Maybe your father has his laptop along?"

She was terrific. Came up with one bright idea after the other. He should be so smart!

"He does," Chris confirmed. "But I'm not allowed to use it."

Fathers are all alike, she mused.

"We could read a book."

"A book? Together? A new trend!" That was funny, but it didn't get them any further.

"Well, if we're about to head home anyway, we don't really need to think of something to do," she said with resignation.

Chris motioned to the veranda, where Simone and Fred Walden had made themselves comfortable with two mugs of coffee.

"They're thinking that over right now."

Chris and Kaya leaned against the kitchen counter and looked outside. The wind was playing with Simone's blonde hair, but that didn't seem to bother her. She gesticulated energetically. Fred Walden listened intently, his head at an angle. Kaya would have loved to know what they were debating out there.

"We could turn on the TV!" Chris pointed at the small television in the corner and the flowery couch and chair in front of it.

"Football?" asked Kaya and meant it as a joke, but Chris nodded earnestly. "That's a great idea!"

She looked him over, but it was clear that he was serious. Did she have to rethink how she felt about him? Was she going to have to spend the weekends getting bored going to football games instead of riding tournaments? He was 15, and who knew what he'd be into at 17, after Wild Thing?

Chris was already at the television and looking for the remote control. Then he plunked himself down on the couch.

Wonderful! And she was left standing there. That guy was certainly overflowing with charm. Annoyed, she stomped off to her room. He should see that she was mad. Her little room was stuffy from the hot morning. She threw open the windows and leaned out. From here she had a perfect view of the clouds and could watch how they rolled in and made the blue sky disappear. She loved clouds. When she was a little kid, she would watch them for hours and look for pictures: a dragon, a giant, a dog's head, a flower, whatever! But now, the only images she could make out were ice cubes stacked on top of each other, and while she thought about that picture, the wind blew a fragment of the conversation on the veranda to her ears.

"In love with him?" That was Mr. Walden. "Well, she'd certainly be a splendid daughter-in-law!"

Were they talking about her?

"Don't be silly! She's thirteen, just a child!"

Now that was mean. She wasn't a kid anymore. She was a teenager and a lot more mature than most people her age. Still, she held her breath and pricked her ears. They were definitely talking about her.

"...need to keep an eye on that..." That was Simone Walden. But now the wind was making too much noise. The first raindrops began to fall and then pattered down so fast that Fred and Simone Walden jumped up and fled into the house. Kaya was deep in thought as she closed the window and then leaned against it.

What if she said that to her son, that Kaya was in love with him? He'd probably laugh himself silly. She had to prevent that at all costs. She had to do something to make them stop thinking that!

She grabbed the first book she could find on the bookshelf and went back to the living room. Mr. and Mrs. Walden stood at the veranda door and looked out at the pouring rain that was coming down in buckets now. Chris had found a sports show on television, but it was only bicycle racing, not football. Kaya didn't care. Both were about as exciting as golf.

Simone Walden turned around to her and asked, "How are your feet doing?"

"Oh thanks, they're feeling better." Since Simone slathered a salve on them and wrapped both feet in thin bandages, they really did feel better. The salve cooled them down and the bandages weren't bulky so her feet fit into her sneakers fine. She had almost forgotten the pain.

"I hardly feel a thing!" she said and got a smile in return.

"You're a tough cookie," said Chris's mother, nodding.

The call came just as the sun broke through the clouds

and the wet earth began to steam. Mr. Miller said that the owner wouldn't go below $65,000, but the examination would be included in that price. Besides, Wild Thing was a guarantee for placing in competitions, had never been sick and was highly cooperative.

"That's true," Fred Walden had to concede. Still he said he needed some time to think it over.

"Dad, she's just perfect!" called Chris from the couch as he jumped up. "She won't go down in value over the next two years!"

Fred Walden poured himself a fresh cup of coffee and nodded. "That's a good point. Of course that's only true if you treat her well and don't injure her!"

Chris went over to him and reached out his hand. "We'll be good!"

His father took it and they shook hands.

Kaya watched them and then felt Simone's gaze on her. Ah yes, she was under observation. She nodded and said in a cool, business-like manner, "I think that the two of them will do well together." Her face was expressionless as she added, "She's certainly a good investment for the future!"

Kaya's father had given her that line when he bought the Hold-o-mat specialty oven for the restaurant kitchen.

Fred Walden said, "If you support Chris, then it'll definitely work out. Dressage isn't Chris's forte, you know."

Kaya beamed. She couldn't hide that. So she was allowed to continue riding Wild Thing? "Is that true?" she asked Chris. "Can I continue to support you?"

He nodded and Kaya gave him a hug. Chris laughed and gave her a little hug, but then she let go of him.

"Sorry," she said to Simone. "I'm just so emotional. That's what my mother's always saying."

"It's nice to see how happy you are!" She gave her husband a peck on his cheek. "I'm happy myself!"

So there they were, standing around in the kitchen like two old couples. Fred Walden asked if they at least had something to drink to make a toast. "We've got to celebrate!" His wife opened the door to the refrigerator and pulled out a bottle of soda, and a beautiful cake, batting her eyelashes and smiling coquettishly.

"Aha," he said and pulled on her ear lobes.

"My goodness, this looks like a conspiracy! Almost as if you knew we'd be buying a horse!"

She laughed. "No, it's no conspiracy, just the result of twenty years of marriage!"

He was confused at first. "Is today our anniversary?"

She passed him the bottle for opening.

"No," she said, "but after twenty years of marriage, you have a pretty good idea of what your partner is going to do, don't you think?"

Mr. Walden nodded quickly and opened the bottle. Kaya helped look around the kitchen for some glasses. She thought that in the past twenty years of marriage, Simone had no doubt studied her husband far more carefully that the other way around.

"Here's to Wild Thing," she said, "and our big success!" The glasses clinked together and the four stood around sipping soda and eating cake.

Then Fred Walden went over to the phone and informed Mr. Miller that he planned to accept the deal. He was told that the mare would be taken to the animal clinic later in the afternoon for the examination.

"That's nice and quick!" said Mr. Walden, appreciatively.

"Then if all goes well, we can soon register her for the next tournaments."

"Exactly. First we'll register as the new owners, then inform the association, and then off to the first course!" Now Chris had to laugh at himself . . . with his big smile and rosy cheeks, he looked like a little kid on Christmas morning. Kaya would have loved to give him another big hug, but because she wanted to be more reserved, she decided to just hold on to her glass instead.

Fred and Simone discussed whether they should go along to the examination and when they should head back home. Chris had gone outside. He obviously wanted to savor this moment alone. Kaya had already put her dishes into the dishwasher and looked over toward where Chris had gone. What should she do?

Chris was busy thinking about his riding future, the Waldens were talking about financial things, and she was alone with herself. Should she call her parents? And what should she tell them? *I'm so lonely, nobody loves me?* Or Alexa? *Chris has a new star pony and I can ride dressage with it now and then?*

She could call her best friend Sina, who didn't understand a thing about horses and just thought they were big and volatile and just totally icky – but what would she say to her? *Chris likes his new pony better than me?*

That was dumb! At this point Kaya just felt blue. And this was supposed to be a celebration!

She was about to go outside when Simone interrupted her thoughts. "Kaya, we'd like to go along to the examination. Didn't you say that you could cook?"

Kaya nodded.

"Could you just make a big pot of spaghetti for us all, with any kind of sauce? Is that something you could manage?"

"Sure," said Kaya, trying to smile. "I'd be happy to."

So that was the deal. She could run across the field like an idiot, wearing her riding boots and getting a ton a blisters just so that she could cook dinner for the lords of the manor. She was nothing more than Cinderella.

She went outside and sat down on the big bench on the side of the house. They should just go and leave her alone here. Fine with her. She'd just go do the cooking.

She looked around.

And where was Chris?

She saw him off in the distance walking around the apple trees, talking on his cell phone. Of course, he had to call all his friends and maybe all his girlfriends, too, and tell them that he just got a National Championship pony and was the greatest.

85

She was already forgotten, sure, and the kiss, too. She grew even more melancholy and began to notice that her limbs were getting heavier and heavier and her head was getting slower and slower. She lay down on the bench and fell asleep.

When she woke up again, she found a note on the
ground next to her. Her back hurt and her right arm
had fallen asleep because she had been lying on it.
She shook it, took a deep breath and looked around.
The evening had a mild, late summer warmth, the
light was muted and she thought she heard the grass
rustle. But that was probably just her imagination.
She sat up and picked up the note.

'Dear Kaya,' she read, 'you were sleeping so
soundly that we didn't want to wake you. Chris
didn't think it was fair for you of all people not to
come along, and we realized then that he was right.
But even he didn't have the heart to wake you from
your deep sleep. So we have gone to the clinic alone,
although I don't really believe that you'll be missing
anything. Enjoy the rest of the afternoon, and if you
feel like – but only if you feel like it – cook some

spaghetti. We expect to be back at about 8 pm. Love from all of us, Simone.'

8 pm? It was only shortly after 6 pm now. And Chris had wanted her to go along? She vowed never again to take naps. Chris had wanted her to go along and she'd lain before him like a newborn baby. Her mouth had probably been open and her face probably looked totally ridiculous. Great!

She got up, angry with herself.

Not quite two hours. It only takes about eight minutes to cook spaghetti. Counting the time it takes for the water to boil and to heat up the sauce, maybe twenty minutes, tops. Was there any salad? What kind of ingredients were there, anyway? If Simone really was such a lousy cook, then she probably only bought cans and mixes. Kaya was in such a foul mood that she hardly recognized herself. If she could have, she would have driven herself home right then and there. Instead, here she was all alone in this silly cabin, all because she fell asleep.

In the kitchen she found some tomato paste and two cans of peeled tomatoes, some spices and a small basil plant in a pot on the windowsill. Okay, that'd be enough for a simple sauce. Salad would be nice, but they didn't have any. Maybe she should go out and pick dandelion greens? They tasted a little like arugula, and if the Waldens didn't know any better, they'd never notice.

Or she could go into town. The stores would probably be open until 6:30 or so, which meant that she'd have to decide quickly. All she needed was money and a bicycle. Her parents had given her $20 just in case and another $20 for her share of the meals, but so far the Waldens had paid for everything. This was her chance to reciprocate.

That was a good idea – she'd reciprocate! Now all she needed was a bicycle. She walked around the cabin and inspected the small wooden shed out back. It looked pretty shabby. The door hung on rusty hinges and squeaked in the most horrible way when she opened it. It had a dirt floor, and the only light came in through a tiny window, but that was enough to allow her to discover a simple black bicycle leaning against the wall – with two flat tires. Drat! If she had found that earlier, then she wouldn't have had to run across the field!

The shed was pretty disgusting, though. Kaya took a deep breath and tried not to get grossed out. She went in and bent over, swishing away the spider webs with her bare hands. She quickly pulled out the bike.

It certainly wasn't the newest of models but, except for the tires, it looked like it was in pretty good shape. It had a basket and even an air pump. Kaya felt her old spirit of adventure coming back. She was ready to conquer the world!

After she pumped up the tires, she took a look at her watch and saw that she had just 15 minutes to find a grocery store. *Okay*, she thought, *go for it, Kaya!* She locked up the cabin, put the keys in the flowerpot, jumped on the bicycle and headed out. The bicycle had wide handlebars and a broad, comfortable seat supported by springs. She rode past the spot of her kiss, but felt like she was above it now and pedaled faster until the springs squeaked and creaked: "quipquap, quipquap." It was a funny sound and she laughed out loud at it. She wouldn't have had much of a chance if she were an Indian on the warpath. She was more like Hannibal riding an elephant.

She rode through the green meadow toward the village. She passed the training center on the right and decided that on the way back she would make a quick stop there. She could watch the experts at work. And who knows? Maybe she would discover a terrific jumper pony that no one wanted anymore because it was too difficult to ride and it would be free for the taking.

Kaya saw herself fighting for a dreamy chestnut mare, one that she would win over with her love. With her pony she'd easily take every hurdle in the world. She would compete against Chris and Wild Thing at the next National Championship tournament and would majestically congratulate Chris and Wild Thing on taking second place. But the flag would be raised for the first place win, for Kaya and her pony. She was so thrilled with her dream that she almost rode right past the little vegetable stand. The bakery on the left and the butcher store on the right were already closed. So they did shut down at 6 pm. It was so annoying out in the country, you never knew if you were too early or too late.

But the standkeeper didn't seem to care about the time and patiently waited on Kaya. She couldn't help herself and, in addition to the salad, she picked out some fresh olives, stuffed grape leaves, sun dried tomatoes and some feta cheese marinated in olive oil. Her mouth was watering, and after she paid she pulled one of the stuffed grape leaves out of the plastic container and took a bite. She loved the taste of the rice stuffing with the leaves and stood next to the bicycle, savoring every bite. That made up for waking up alone. After she licked off each of her fingers, she tucked her bag of goodies into the basket and swung her leg onto the bicycle.

Life was great, she was happy and she knew that she would get ahead. Whatever it took, she would succeed. With this feeling in her heart, she headed back and looked at every hill as a wonderful new challenge. When her feet started burning again, she told them that you had to make certain sacrifices to achieve your goal. She thought about what the biggest sacrifice was for her right now – and decided that it was the lack of a motor on the bicycle!

Kaya was sweaty and extremely thirsty by the time she reached the riding hall. Driving in the car she hadn't notice how hilly this area really was. First she needed something to drink, and then she'd have a closer look at the set-up inside.

She parked her bicycle with all the delicacies in the basket a little out of the way, behind one of the longeing arenas. She planned to whip up a luxurious dinner for everyone tonight and couldn't risk anything happening to her purchases. Even out in the boondocks there were thieves, she was sure of that.

She was in a great mood as she strode into the huge riding arena with the adjacent stabling. Again she heard the deafening sound of birds chirping. She found it quite strange. Wasn't the nesting season over already? Or did these birds breed twice a year? She'd have to ask her biology teacher about that when school was back in session, or she could check it on the Internet. Were swallows constant breeders? Was there such a thing?

There were four big horses in the riding hall. One of them floated along the diagonal with a fast trot. It was unbelievable how such huge, heavy horses could do that. They looked like they were dancing gracefully, as if they didn't even have to touch the ground. Kaya watched happily. It was beautiful to see, even if she couldn't do that herself. *But just you wait, Kaya*, she said to herself, *you want to get ahead and you'll be able to do that, too. One of these days, you'll be sitting here on one of these magnificent animals.*

With this feeling of certainty, she began looking around the stables. She saw a water faucet and was tempted to turn it on to slake her thirst. She looked around, but didn't see anyone nearby. She figured what was good for the horses couldn't hurt her. She opened the faucet and drank the water from her cupped hand and then turned it off again. Well, that was a good start! Then she walked on. The stalls were roomy, with plenty of straw on the ground, and each horse had its own big window. The names of each of the horses were printed on elegant signs, and Kaya began to read through the breeding history of each stall resident. Not that she knew much about that, really. She had heard about some of the top studs, but most of the stallion names meant nothing at all to her. *No big deal*, she thought; *you're only 13 and have plenty of time to learn*. She zigzagged through the stable and looked at each horse and its name. Sprite and Angelique, Danger, Hurricane, Highlight, Lucky Lady, Feeling, Florian, Dancer, Dentano, Nike, Ta Karou, El Matador – there was no end. Then there were a few slate boards on which the respective horse names were only written in chalk. Aha, these must be the horses who were boarding for training or who were up for sale. With any luck, she'd now find the pony she had been dreaming of. She grinned to herself. Maybe she had too active an imagination – although her English teacher always gave her poor marks in composition. "Did not address the topic adequately" or "too far afield of assignment." And then a depressing grade. She stopped in front of Gardeur, an elegant chestnut with blue eyes. She found it so unusual, that she had to take a closer look to be sure that she wasn't dreaming. What was that about? Suddenly she thought she heard someone sobbing. But she was alone here; there was no other person to be seen. But then she heard it again. She held her breath. Was she imagining it? It couldn't be the chestnut in front of her. That would be a true sensation: a crying horse! And she would be Mrs. Doolittle. Now all he had to do was tell her why he was crying. But seriously, where was that sobbing coming from?

She looked around, looked up and down the passageway, and then noticed that one of the stall doors had only been leaned closed. She gingerly walked up to it, trying not to make a sound. And sure enough, that strange noise was the sound of sobbing, and it was getting louder. She hesitated for a minute and then suddenly had to sneeze. Now of all times. Three sneezes in a row.

For a minute it was silent. Kaya was rooted to the spot. Nothing moved, and just as she was ready to turn around, a girl poked her head out of the stall door.

They looked at each other, neither saying a word. But then Kaya noticed the red eyes and tear-stained face. She figured the girl was a little older than herself, maybe as old as Alexa, 17 or so. The other girl pulled her head back in and Kaya looked at the spot where it had just been. She couldn't just let it go at that.

She took one step forward, then another until she reached that stall. She looked in. The girl was standing, leaning on the back wall. She wiped under her nose with the back of her hand.

"I have a tissue if you need one," said Kaya quietly. She almost started crying herself. Her mother was right, she really was ridiculously emotional. The girl nodded.

She had wavy, dark brown hair a little longer than shoulder length, and hazel brown eyes. She wore jeans, not riding clothes.

Kaya fumbled for the crumpled tissue she had in her pants pocket and reached it over to the other girl. She rubbed her eyes with it, which only made her look worse. Finally, she stuffed the tissue in her pocket and looked at Kaya.

"Nicole," she said.

"Kaya."

It was quiet again.

"Do you need help with something?" Kaya asked carefully.

At first the other girl said nothing, but then she broke into tears again. Sobbing, she turned around and leaned against the wall with her head between her folded arms. At first Kaya just watched her, but then she couldn't take it anymore. She walked over to Nicole and put her hand on her back.

"My pony is gone!" she heard her say in between sobs.

"What? Your pony is gone?" Kaya began stroking her back. Nicole was bigger and broader than she was, and she could feel her muscles through her T-shirt. "But where could it have gone?"

Now Nicole turned around and with her back against the wall, slid down into a squat. Kaya squatted in the straw next to her.

"Did it run away?"

Nicole shook her head.

"My father sold it and now it's gone. I didn't even get to see it one last time. And I don't even know who he sold it to!"

"What do you mean, you don't know who he sold it to? If your father sold your pony, then he must know the new owner!"

"Mr. Miller sold it for us and he said that the new owner isn't interested in knowing the former owner. All he's interested in is the pony!"

Kaya looked at her, dumbfounded. "There are

people like that?" she asked. "What kind of people would be that way?"

Nicole sat down in the straw, her arms on her knees. She didn't say anything.

"If I only knew!" she said after a while, "but I don't. That's the problem. And now my pony is gone and I couldn't even say goodbye, don't know where she's gone, how she's doing and if the new owner will even love her..."

She broke out in tears again and Kaya almost cried along with her. The thought of it was awful! She couldn't bear to imagine it.

"But why did your father sell to people like that? You can't let people like that have your pony," she concluded quietly. If she had a father like that, she'd kill him.

"But he didn't know! It all happened so quickly. Mr. Miller called us this afternoon and said she was sold and gone." She looked at her tissue. "And I got here too late."

Kaya raised her head.

"Wait a minute!" She thought for a minute and then wiped under her own nose with the back of her hand. "What did you sell your pony for?"

"How much? My father wanted sixty, but fifty is what he got." She gave Kaya a strange look. "Thousand."

"Fifty thousand dollars?" asked Kaya. Nicole nodded.

"Oh," said Kaya. "Too bad."

"What do you mean?" asked Nicole.

"Because friends of mine bought a pony today for $65,000."

Nicole nodded slowly. "No, then it can't be mine. That's what my father originally wanted – actually he wanted $70,000, but Mr. Miller said that she wasn't worth that anymore. Wild Thing had navicular disease and had a neurectomy to treat it. That lowered her value."

"Wild Thing?" Kaya was flabbergasted. "You mean *the* Wild Thing?"

Nicole squinted at her. "You don't mean to tell me you know Wild Thing, do you?"

"I don't believe it." Kaya slapped her thighs. "How much did you say? That's just impossible."

Nicole looked at her blankly. "I don't understand what you're trying to say."

"But I'm just starting to understand myself!"

"Then explain it to me, please!"

"Is that Wild Thing's stall?"

Nicole nodded.

"And you rode her, placed in the National Championships and just turned 17?"

Nicole nodded again.

Kaya held out her hand. "Give me five! This is a surprise. Come with me. I know where your pony is and I'll take you to the new owners. I'm sure they'll be extremely happy to meet you, guaranteed! And then some."

Nicole slapped her hand.

"Really?" she said doubtfully.

"But first, it would be best if you called your father. He should come along, too."

"Why? Where are we going?"

"I'll tell you that later!"

"But why?"

"Because we are going to save the day!"

Nicole set the table while Kaya worked at the stove. She stirred the two pots, a big one filled with spaghetti in boiling water and smaller one with sauce.

"I just can't believe it. He can't do that!" said Nicole once again. "I can't believe I ever trusted him!"

"Greed is a powerful thing!" Kaya turned around and tried to give her a cynical grin. "That's always the way, isn't it? Wherever there's big money to be had, honesty goes out the window!" That line was from her mother. Kaya was tired of hearing it, but it fit perfectly in this situation. Hit the nail on the head.

"I suppose you're right." Nicole looked around. "What about napkins?"

"No idea. Does the table have a drawer? Maybe in there?"

Nicole found a stack of pink napkins with roses. Obviously left behind by the last guests.

"Now isn't that adorable!" Kaya arranged the appetizers that she had bought from the grocer in little bowls and decorated the table with them. She set the table with flowered glasses and even found a few candles that she lit. Then she gave the table one last critical inspection.

"What do you think?" she asked Nicole, who reminded her of her older sister.

"Are you in the business, or something?" asked Nicole. "You did all this like a pro."

"Oh thanks!" Kaya tried to think of an appropriate answer, but behind her back she heard the hiss of the stove as the pot of spaghetti boiled over and she turned around quickly to deal with it.

Simone Walden came in first. She was so surprised by what she saw that she stopped abruptly at the threshold and her husband bumped right into her. "Zowie!" she said and stared at the table Kaya had set. "Can we adopt you?"

Kaya had to laugh, and then she introduced Nicole. "This is Nicole, she helped me out."

"Oh, a visitor!" Simone walked to the middle of the room so that her husband and Chris could also come in. She held out her hand to Nicole. "How nice! How did you two meet?"

"We'll explain that in a minute," said Kaya, waving aside the question. "More importantly, though, how did it go?" She watched Chris shake hands with Nicole. If she turned out to be his type, then there'd be trouble. But he was too excited to pay much attention to the new girl.

"First class! She got a clean bill of health!" he said to Kaya and gave her a playful box on her arm. "Wild Thing is in excellent shape, through and through. She sailed through every test with flying colors!"

"Then the veterinarian is a fraud!" said Nicole. Everyone turned and gaped at her.

"A fraud?" said Chris skeptically. "What is that supposed to mean?"

"It means that Wild Thing had a neurectomy, front right. It was performed after she developed navicular disease and the vet knows that perfectly well. But I suppose if you're the stable vet to so many horses, then you have to make certain compromises."

"What?" Now Fred Walden was taking notice. "What is that supposed to mean?"

Nicole pointed out the window. "There's my father coming up the walkway. He can explain the whole thing to you."

That's when Simone Walden noticed that the table was set for six people.

Kaya took the spaghetti out of the water.

"They're going to be totally soft," she complained to herself, but no one was thinking about food right then. Everyone sat down at the table and grabbed at the appetizers – and couldn't believe what they were hearing from Nicole's Dad.

"He told us that the owner wouldn't accept less than $65,000 and that was his last offer."

"And he told us that with the neurectomy, there was no way to ask for more than $50,000, that more wasn't justified – and that it was immoral to ask for a higher price!"

"Immoral! Ha!" said Simone. "We wanted to meet the owner, because that would help us get to know the pony better. We don't want to make any mistakes when it comes to food, care, allergies, and so on. But he said the owner wanted nothing to do with the buyer!"

Nicole nodded bitterly. "And he told us that the buyer wasn't interested in having any contact, and that the pony was being taken out of state."

"And the difference is exactly $15,000, money under the table instead of the usual commission. What a rotten person!" Nicole's father was genuinely shaken. He was a much burlier man than Fred Walden. With his brawny biceps, he looked like a former prizefighter. "Miller had better hope that I don't get my hands on him anytime soon!"

Fred Walden looked at him. "Oh I believe that!" he said. Then he hesitated and said, "Althooooough . . ."

"Yes, that's right!" Simone looked from one man to the other.

"Both of you need to go to him tomorrow and confront him with this story. After all, as a state trainer, he's supposed to be a role model. Some role model. He's as corrupt as a politician."

Her husband laughed. "But we're smarter!" he said.

"What do you mean 'we'?" Chris wrinkled his forehead. "Without Kaya, you would have paid $65,000 and Mr. Rose would have gotten his $50,000 and no one would have been any the wiser!"

"That's true!"

Now everyone looked at Kaya, who looked smaller and smaller. She needed to put the spaghetti back in hot water or it'd be totally cold. Or maybe she should make a fresh batch? But wasn't that a big waste?

They were all still looking at her.

"What are we going to do now?" Fred asked Mr. Rose. "Do I pay $65,000 or $50,000?"

Mr. Rose looked at Nicole. "Wild Thing had a neurectomy. Have you considered that?"

"Well, now we know it," answered Fred Walden. "And I know a few ponies who are still happily leaping around, despite a neurectomy." He looked at his wife, then at Chris and then at his wife again. "Does this change our decision?" Both shook their heads.

"Can Nicole visit Wild Thing every so often?" Mr. Rose asked and got a loving smile from his daughter.

"She can even ride her!" said Chris, smiling.

Ouch, thought Kaya.

"After all, she's not some inexperienced beginner!" he added. Now he got a loving smile from Nicole.

Kaya took a deep breath.

"But naturally only if Kaya gives her consent!" Now she got a tender smile. From Chris. She blushed almost instantaneously. She could have slapped herself. "Of course I do!" she said quickly.

They were all looking at her again. And again, she wished she could slip out and deal with the spaghetti.

"We could meet in the middle, then each of us has some benefit from all this," suggested Fred Walden.

"That would be $57,500," Mr. Rose calculated out loud.

"Wouldn't we like to have dinner first?" Simone Walden pointed at Kaya. "She worked so hard on it and if we just sit here talking and talking, then the whole thing will burn to a crisp. And that would be a crying shame!"

Kaya and Nicole jumped up at the same time, and when they reached the stove, Nicole gave her a loud kiss on the cheek.

"I'll never forget you for this!" she said. "You really saved me. I don't know what I would have done if Wild Thing just disappeared from my life. Thank you soooo much!"

Both girls were moved and tried to hide it by hugging each other. As they pulled apart, Kaya glanced over at Simone Walden, who was watching her with a warm expression in her eyes. Then she quietly said something to her husband, who responded by nodding thoughtfully.

Kaya couldn't make rhyme or reason out of that, so she put it out of her head and focused on heating up the spaghetti sauce again. She threw a new batch of spaghetti into a pot of boiling water and stood next to the stove to wait for the pasta to be cooked *al dente* this time instead of mushy.

She was endlessly happy over this turn of events. If she hadn't fallen asleep, then she wouldn't have found Nicole and everything would have turned out completely differently.

Her mother always said that sometimes, when you're really down and desperately sad, and it looks as if there's no way out of a situation, then suddenly things happen that change the situation completely. So far that never did happen with stuff in school, and it didn't happen with Chris either. But maybe now she had just reached that point where something like that was possible. Who knew? She got caught up in her own thoughts and didn't pay attention to the others. All she did was fish out a piece of spaghetti from the boiling water to test if it was done. Suddenly she felt so mature.

They ate every last bit of food. There was no more sauce and all of them had scraped their plates clean. The olives had been eaten and even the stale rolls from the morning had been eaten. Happily well fed, Mr. Rose and the Waldens were on a first name basis. Chris, Nicole and Kaya were disappointed that they couldn't cap off their night by going out dancing, since there was no disco in this little town. Suddenly Fred Walden clinked his knife against his water glass.

Everyone looked at him and stopped talking. For a moment the room was totally silent. Then he stood up, looked from one person to another until finally his gaze landed festively on Kaya. She felt small again and didn't know where to look.

"My dear Kaya," he began. "I must tell you that you have really brought us good luck!" Kaya felt herself blush again. "Not only because you are such a good rider," he continued, "who protects our son when he does something foolish," he fixed his eyes on Chris who grinned cheekily. "But you are truly an exceptional girl – and on top of it all, you're a good cook!"

Now he looked at Simone. "If you were a little older, I'd accept you as a daughter-in-law in a heartbeat!"

Kaya shrunk down in her chair more and more. She quickly looked at Chris. He was still smiling. "But you're just 13, still discovering the world, you are circumspect, brave and self confident. Bravo!"

"Bravo!" said Mr. Rose, too.

"And because of that, you discovered a fraud against people and an animal. And more than that – you prevented it. You deserve a medal!"

"That's for sure!" said Nicole.

"But because we don't have any medals, and maybe because there's something else you can put to better use, Simone and I have decided the following, as long as William also agrees."

"I agree!" said Mr. Rose.

Again there was a brief pause and Kaya felt how every hair on her body was standing on end from all the excitement. What would happen next?

"Good! Since William agrees, it's my opinion that we meet each other halfway with the price, and that each of us sets aside 10% of the amount that we saved, so even though I'll be paying Mr. Rose $57,500, we'll each give you a commission of $1500. Because if it weren't for you, it would have turned out much worse for both of us!"

"Good idea!" Mr. Rose agreed and everyone nodded. Except for Kaya, who didn't understand a single thing. Helplessly, she looked at Chris. "What's going on?" she asked quietly.

He laughed loudly, then stood up and walked around the table to her, pulled her up out of her seat and hugged her.

"I think you just earned three thousand bucks!" he said loudly and planted a kiss on her cheek as everyone cheered. "And you really deserve it." When he let go of her, Kaya sank into her chair, dazed.

"Three thousand dollars?" she asked. "But why?"

"Because you truly earned the money!" said Simone, smiling. She got up herself to take Kaya into her arms. "And because you need new riding boots! And maybe you're saving for a pony of your own?"

A pony of her own? She pictured herself as she zoomed down the hill on her bicycle. Hadn't she foretold it? That was just a few hours ago, and now look what had happened.

"Thank you, thank you so much!!!!" she cheered and wiped under her nose with the back of her hand. "I don't know what to say to all this!" She looked into each face, so happy and full of expectation, and then shook her head.

"I'm sorry, I just can't find the right words to say!"

"How about: HAPPY ENDING?" said Chris as he gave her a wink.

More adventures with Kaya!

Kaya is 13 years old and loves horses more than
anything and she loves her pony, Flying Dream,
most of all. Paradise is her small stable, where she
and her friends spend their best times together.
Unfortunately her parents aren't aware of most
of this because they are too busy running their
restaurant. To the surprise of everyone, Kaya, riding
Dreamy, takes third place at a big riding tournament.
A dream come true! But her success with Dreamy
makes others interested in her pony and now
Dreamy is suddenly up for sale. Kaya thinks it's
unfair and thinks about kidnapping – horsenapping.
Meanwhile, Chris, the boy she has a crush on,
seems to be interested in older girls. That's not at all
acceptable. So Kaya comes up with some wild plans
and the adventures begin . . .

Volume 1: *Kaya Does It Her Way*

Still more adventures with Kaya!

At the stable, the girls are in the middle of a dress rehearsal for the Christmas pageant when the police call. Five horses have been sighted running loose on a rural road outside of town. They ask the experts from the stable to bring them in and shelter them until the owner is found. Kaya, the 13-year-old Amazon, spontaneously decides to join the search team that Claudia, her riding teacher, is organizing. Together they go out in the dark, snowy night to catch the animals. When they find the horses, they see that they are malnourished and utterly neglected – and why, they wonder, has no one reported the loss of the horses? Where do they come from? There's something fishy here, and Kaya and her friends set out to find out just what it is...

Volume 3: *Kaya Keeps Her Cool*